# FIRST FLIGHT®

*FIRST FLIGHT® is an exciting new series of beginning readers.
The series presents titles which include songs,
poems, adventures, mysteries, and humor
by established authors and illustrators.
FIRST FLIGHT® makes the introduction to reading fun
and satisfying for the young reader.*

*FIRST FLIGHT® is available in 4 levels
to correspond to reading development.*

**Level 1 – Preschool - Grade 1**
Large type, repetition of simple concepts that are perfect for reading aloud,
easy vocabulary and endearing characters in short simple
stories for the earliest reader.

**Level 2 – Grade 1 - Grade 3**
Longer sentences, higher level of vocabulary, repetition, and
high-interest stories for the progressing reader.

**Level 3 – Grade 2 - Grade 4**
Simple stories with more involved plots and a simple chapter format
for the newly independent reader.

**Level 4 – Grade 3 - up (First Flight Chapter Books)**
More challenging level, minimal illustrations for the independent reader.

### First four books in the First Flight series

**Level 1 • Fishes in the Ocean *written by* Maggee Spicer
*and* Richard Thompson, *illustrated by* Barbara Hartmann**

**Level 2• Jingle Bells *written and illustrated by* Maryann Kovalski**

**Level 3 • Andrew's Magnificent Mountain of Mittens
*written by* Deanne Lee Bingham, *illustrated by* Kim LaFave**

**Level 4 • The Money Boot *written by* Ginny Russell,
*illustrated by* John Mardon**

# THE MONEY BOOT

FIRST FLIGHT® is a registered trademark of Fitzhenry and Whiteside

First publication in the United States in 1999.

Fitzhenry & Whiteside acknowledges with thanks the support of the
Government of Canada through its Book Publishing Industry
Development Program in the publication of this title.

Printed in Canada.
Cover Design by Wycliffe Smith.
Cover Illustration: John Mardon.

10 9 8 7 6 5 4 3

Canadian Cataloguing in Publication Data

Russell, Ginny, 1931-
The money boot

(A first flight chapter book)
ISBN 1-55041-370-8

I. Mardon, John. II. Title. III. Series.

PS8585.U767M66 1998     jC813'.54     C98-931737-4
PZ7.R87Mo 1998

**A First Flight Level Four Reader**

# THE MONEY BOOT

By Ginny Russell
Illustrated by John Mardon

Fitzhenry and Whiteside • Toronto

# [ CHAPTER ONE ]

"Some Christmas Holidays," grumbled Jim. "What's the good of new skates if you can't use them. It's not fair!"

"Maybe tomorrow," said Mom, patting his head. "I think your ankle will be better by then."

"Too bad about the skates, Jim," said Dad gently, as he put on his coat. "See you later. Don't forget to watch me run to the corner."

Jim raced to the kitchen window. He loved to watch his father make the morning dash. In less than a minute Dad could run all the way to the subway station.

"Rats," said Jim, "kitchen window's all frozen. I can't see anything." Angrily, he scraped a small peep hole through the frost. Dad had long since disappeared down the subway stairs. Jim gazed at the streets below. He lived on the seventh floor of his apartment building. He had a clear view of the people hurrying across the road when the traffic lights changed.

Today everyone scurried faster than ever in a world of white flurries. It had been snowing hard for three days. Two yellow snow ploughs on the main street were busy pushing the snow into towering piles. The wind was busy too, picking up snow and blowing it back, scattering it on the streets and walkways. Sometimes the wind blew in circles, creating swirling puffballs, chasing people across the busy intersections.

Even inside his warm apartment, Jim could hear the wind howl. He could feel it rattling the kitchen window.

It made him shiver but he kept his nose pressed hard against the glass.

"At least we can watch the hockey game," said his mother cheerily. "Don't you remember who's playing tonight?"

"Leafs and Rangers!" shouted Jim, happy now. "I was feeling so down in the dumps, I forgot."

Jim climbed up on a kitchen stool. He had to help his mother find the family recipe for butterscotch fudge.

Tonight, Jim and his family would enjoy the fudge that he and his mother made, while the Toronto Maple Leafs played the New York Rangers.

As the TV announcers would shout, "he shoots, he scores," sticky fingers would devour butterscotch fudge while each family member cheered for their favorite players. It was a Kovach family tradition.

"We'll make the fudge at lunch time," Mom promised. "I've got some work to finish first." She had a computer in the big bedroom and did office work at home. Dozens of letters had to be written and mailed today.

"Maybe one of your pals can come over to play," suggested Mom, as she closed the bedroom door firmly.

Jim telephoned five friends. Not one was home, and Jim felt very lonely. 'It's just me against the world,' he decided sadly. Curling up in Dad's big chair, he reached for the new mystery book his friend Gary had given him for Christmas.

# [ CHAPTER TWO ]

*The Case of the Missing Microchip* was so exciting, Jim read it straight through from beginning to end. Then it was nearly noon. Jim's stomach said, "lunch time," but Mom was still busy. If he made the lunch, Mom would have more time to make the butter-scotch fudge, wouldn't she?

Jim found some left over Christmas turkey in the refrigerator and made sandwiches. "Bless you, dear," said his mother, when she sat down at the table.

As soon as they'd finished eating, it was time to make the candy. Jim put all the ingredients out on the counter. "Butter, brown sugar, white sugar, salt, corn syrup, milk, vanilla," he chanted, as he checked the recipe again.

The writing was hard for Jim to decipher. And that wasn't the only problem. The little yellow card was torn at the edges, covered with sticky spots and smeared with melted butter. Jim and his mother pretty much knew the recipe by heart, but consulting the original instructions was part of the ritual of candy making.

Jim did the mixing, but Mom had to stir the candy once it started to boil because bubbling hot fudge can sometimes spatter. "Ummm, it smells better than ever," sighed Jim, as Mom finally poured it into a pan.

Soon the fudge had hardened and was cool enough to taste. Each of the two cooks tried a tiny square. Then another one, just to make absolutely sure. Yes, it tasted just as good as it smelled.

Jim and his Mom decided to make a second batch. Tonight's hockey game might go into overtime. It could be a long late evening. "Should be a great game," sighed Jim happily as he measured out the ingredients once more. "New York's in first place, but I think we can beat 'em."

"I bet you and your dad will make short work of this fudge," chuckled Mom, as she hurried back to her desk. She still had many more letters to write.

Jim thought of the puzzle his father had given him for Christmas. Each year the puzzle he received got bigger. This year's offering said eight hundred pieces on the side of the box.

"This is a grown up puzzle," Jim complained to himself. "And it's got skaters in the picture." Remembering the fact that he could not use his shiny new skates made Jim sad all over again.

"Never mind," he told himself, "I'm going to do this puzzle." It would pass the time, and Jim wanted to prove to his parents that he could do it. He would finish the puzzle, even if it took him from now until New Year's Day.

Two and a half hours later, Jim had all the edge pieces in place. "I deserve a break," he decided. He made two big mugs of hot chocolate and called Mom. She gave him a hug and admired his work.

"I'll be finished in half an hour," she promised. "Then I can help."

The wind rattled hard against the kitchen window and Jim ran over to peer outside. The glass was frosted over in one large, lacy, leafy set of white crystals. Jim scraped a clear space with his thumbnail. What could he see?

# [ CHAPTER THREE ]

It was beginning to get dark outside, and the light inside the apartment was fading too. Jim turned on the lamp in the kitchen and then hurried back to his kitchen window peep hole, hoping to see his father. Dad worked in a coffee and doughnut shop that closed at four o'clock sharp. If Dad didn't stop to buy groceries, he'd be home soon.

All across the darkening city, street lights blinked to life. The snow had stopped falling. The air was clean and clear. Jim could see all the way to the nearest stores and a huge outdoor Christmas tree, twinkling with lights. He was glad that no one had taken the tree down yet.

From his eagle's perch, Jim could see far beyond the shops and the gigantic tree, all the way to the tall towers of the downtown office buildings. Their lighted windows made a warm gleam in the distance.

Below, Jim watched the moving lights as thousands of cars and buses crisscrossed the city streets.Rush hour had begun. The main roads were moving ribbons of white and red. One ribbon was bumper to bumper headlights. Another was bumper to bumper taillights. Jim stared out at the scene.

A few floors below, electrical power lines twanged as the wind whipped bare tree branches against the wires. A gusty gale whistled through the tunnel between apart-ment buildings on either side of the narrow street. "It's like a canyon," thought Jim, "the windiest canyon in Toronto."

Jim wasn't surprised when the light in his kitchen flickered and dimmed. "What do you bet the power goes off right at the beginning of the hockey game," he called out to his Mom.

Maybe he should turn on the lights of their very own Christmas tree? That would certainly be a cheerful sight before the power went off. How about the radio? Jim wanted to catch the weather forecast.

"The coldest, windiest December 27th on record, a really frosty Friday," joked the weather reporter. Jim thought her voice sounded like she was shivering. "Here in Toronto, it was minus 23 at three o'clock. Tomorrow should be much warmer all along the north shore of Lake Ontario. Watch out for frostbite, folks. With this strong wind you can freeze your nose in two minutes."

"This window's got a bad case of frostbite," muttered Jim. He was still trying to scratch a bigger peep hole, when he heard a loud knock at the door.

# [ CHAPTER FOUR ]

"It's me," called a familiar voice.

"Gary?" Jim threw the door open wide. "Come on in! I thought you were in New York for the holidays!"

"We went early and came home early. Got back a few minutes ago."

"Wow, Gary! I see you got what you wanted for Christmas!" Jim said pointing at Gary's sweater.

"Yeah, my New York Rangers hockey sweater. Awesome, eh? I've only been hinting for two years. Oh, thanks for the hockey socks, Jim."

"And thanks for *The Case of the Missing Microchip*," said Jim. "It was so good, I finished it in one gulp. Want to borrow it?"

"Well, actually, I read it before I wrapped it up," admitted Gary with a grin. "Hey, Jim, did you get your new skates?"

"Yeah, there they are, beside the front door. But I fell on the ice yesterday. Hurt my ankle. Didn't even get around the rink once."

"Tough luck!"

"Mom says I can try again tomorrow. Hey, now that you're home, we can go together!" Jim was glad that his friend was home. Gary was a good skater and a good friend. He didn't laugh when Jim fell down on the ice, which happened quite often. Gary had moved to Toronto a year ago and the two boys had been pals ever since. Gary even lived in the same apartment building, on the ninth floor, two floors above Jim.

"Want to see what else I got for Christmas?" asked Gary, peering at Jim over his glasses. Jim was never sure exactly why Gary wore glasses, because every time he talked to anyone, he always looked over his lenses instead of through them.

"See. It's a great magnifying glass!" boasted Gary. "Grandpa Ishida gave it to me. He got it when he was a kid and he brought it with him from Japan. Now it's mine. And Grandpa gave me all these old coins for my collection. See, these ones are Japanese and the others are Spanish." Jim peered at the money through Gary's magnifying glass while Gary was busy inspecting the pile of presents that still lay under Jim's Christmas tree.

"I see you've got a new flashlight," said Gary. "To little Jimmy from Uncle Albert."

"Nuts to Uncle Albert," complained Jim. "I hate being called little Jimmy, and this flashlight's got no batteries." He shook it in disgust. "Mom says I have to save up for them. All I've got is seventy two cents."

"Money doesn't grow on trees," came Mom's muffled shout from the next room. "Isn't that what Uncle Albert always says?"

"Grandpa Ishida says that too," Gary shouted back. "Let's have a look at the flashlight, Jim. I heard something rattling inside." He unscrewed the end.

"Aha," shrieked Gary. "Your Uncle Albert's pretty tricky!"

# [ CHAPTER FIVE ]

Gary pulled out two crisp new bills from inside the flashlight, one for five dollars and the other for two. "Five dollars should be enough for a couple of batteries," he suggested.

Jim was pleased. "I can keep the two dollars for a souvenir. They don't make bills any more, now that we've got two dollar coins. Good old Uncle Albert," he chuckled. "Hey Mom, can I test my ankle? It feels OK. We need to go to the store. Uncle Albert sent money for the batteries."

"Wellllllll, all right dear, as long as you two stay together. Your flashlight might come in handy, if the power goes off. But you'll have to bundle up. The cold will take your breath away."

Gary went upstairs to find his outdoor clothing and the two boys met in the front lobby. Jim had stuffed the flashlight into his pocket so that he'd be sure to buy the right size batteries. Each boy wore his warmest boots, heaviest winter clothes and each had a thick woolen scarf around his neck.

Outside, the wind was even fiercer than Jim imagined. He and Gary pulled their hats down to their eyebrows, and their scarves up over their noses. They could barely see through the narrow slits that remained.

The boys trudged along rapidly, snow swirling around their legs, blowing up into their faces and filling their footprints as soon as they made them. It whipped the naked trees overhead, dropping scores of small broken branches across the snow covered sidewalk.

Jim's ankle seemed to be fine and they walked as fast as they could. The penetrating cold made it hard to breathe, and impossible to talk. They plodded on silently, straight into the wind, scarves pulled tight, mittened hands wedged firmly into pockets.

Their own steamy breath kept their mouths and noses warm.

It was nearly half an hour before they came to the neighbourhood corner store where the tall Christmas tree glittered with its icy ornaments of silver and blue. Jim could hear sharp rattling and tinkling sounds as the wind whistled through the branches. "Looks like the tree's shivering too," he said, as his teeth chattered.

The boys burst into the small grocery store, glad to be indoors. Unfortunately the store had not one battery left! The two friends tramped out, crossed the street to the drug store and stumbled inside. Perhaps they'd be luckier this time.

The store was warm. Cheerful music filled the air, and so did the smell of perfumed soap. Gary's glasses fogged up, but he didn't mind. They relaxed, lowered their scarves, pushed up their hats and strolled up and down the aisles for a long time until a clerk finally cornered them.

"What do you boys want?" she asked suspiciously.

"Two batteries, size C?" asked Jim, hopefully, waving his five dollar bill.

"My last two," said the clerk, plunking them down on the counter. "We had them on sale today, two for the price of one. I sold dozens of flashlights and candles too. Folks must be worried about power failure. Here, sonny, I'll put the batteries in the flashlight. Now you boys hurry home, before you turn into icicles!"

Jim thanked the clerk and counted his change. "Look, Gary," he said happily, "with the money I had already, we've got enough to take the subway home and still not use my two dollar bill!"

"It's only one stop," protested Gary. "We never take the subway for one stop! But... you're right. It's a great idea," he agreed hastily. "Come on, Jim. I'll race you, before you change your mind!"

# [ CHAPTER SIX ]

Jim and Gary covered their faces again and set off to catch the subway train. The wind was at their backs and a big help. In less than a minute, it blew them straight into the station.

Inside the crowded subway car, slushy snow melted from people's boots. The floor was one huge puddle. The air was so warm and moist, that Gary's glasses steamed up again, blinding him. Jim had to lead him by the hand when it was time to get off the train.

"Have you decided what to write for your school story next week?" asked Jim as they walked along.

"What I did on my Christmas vacation? No, not yet," answered Gary. "We still have a few days. How about you Jim?"

"I'm hoping that something really exciting will happen," said Jim, as he pulled Gary onto the subway station's UP escalator.

Suddenly all the lights went out, except for a few emergency flashers. The escalator stopped with a jerk. The boys stumbled up the stalled steps and pushed open the heavy glass doors leading to the street.

All was dark. There were no friendly street lights. Houses and apartment buildings were black shapes in the darkness, and traffic snarled because the crossing lights at the busy intersection were out. Drivers honked impatiently.

Headlights were the only light in the dark gloom. It was only by using the glow from the cars stuck in traffic that the boys could tell where the sidewalk ended and the roadway began. They stood at the corner with a large crowd, waiting for a break.

"Not far to go now," said Jim. "My Dad runs it in less than a minute. Even walking in this snow, we can do it in five minutes."

# [ CHAPTER SEVEN ]

It took Jim and Gary much longer than five minutes to walk from the subway to their apartment building. Just as the boys began to cross the street, the woman in front of them slipped on a patch of ice and fell. The boys tripped over her. Other people tumbled on top of them.

"Can I help you?" Jim asked the woman, after he had untangled himself from the heap. He reached out with his hand. The woman ignored Jim and stood up by herself.

"Don't need your help!" she huffed gruffly. The woman's face was so wrapped in scarves, the boys could not see her eyes. She hugged her shopping bags close to her body and hurried on ahead. She walked in a very strange way, more like a shuffle, as if her boots might fall off as she picked up her feet.

"Perhaps she's wearing her husband's boots by mistake," whispered Gary.

Jim studied the wobbly walker in front of them. "Maybe her own boots were stolen," he whispered, "and somebody loaned her a pair so she could get home."

"Maybe," agreed Gary. "Your guess is as good as mine."

Jim dug his flashlight out of his pocket and shone it on the sidewalk in front of him. "Look, we can follow her, because the wind is dying down. The snow is not filling up our footprints like it did when we started out."

"She's dragging one foot," decided Gary. "Maybe she hurt her ankle and she really needs help. Uh-oh. Which way did she go at the corner? We've lost the trail."

"There's her tracks turning onto our street," whispered Jim. He and Gary kept their eyes on the huge boot prints ahead of them. The trail wasn't difficult to follow now. The marks from the dragging left boot were unmistakable. Soon, the boys caught sight of a shuffling figure ahead of them and they weren't surprised when the figure tripped and muttered some coarse words.

"It's her, I'm sure," said Gary. "She must have dropped her shopping bags. I heard them crackle." When the boys caught up with the woman, she lay sprawled on the ground, her parcels scattered around her. Before they had time to offer their help, she waved them away.

"Leave me alone," she barked sharply as she struggled to her feet. Gathering her plastic bags, she waddled on faster than before. Jim still had his flashlight turned on and he noticed something sparkling on the snow.

"Hey, lady," he called, "you dropped some money. It's right here under this little cedar tree."

"Wow," gasped Gary. "Remember what your Uncle and my Grandpa always say about money?"

"What? Oh, you mean money doesn't grow on trees. But how about under?" Hearing the boys excited chatter, the woman slowed down and even stood still for a moment. She muttered quietly to herself, and finally started off again.

"Why doesn't she come back?" Jim wondered.

"Beats me," said Gary. "I'm sure she heard us. Shine your light down here again, we might as well pick these up," he said as he gathered up two handfuls of ice cold coins and stuffed them inside his mitten.

"Here we are! Home at last!" said Jim. But just as he spoke, he stumbled, falling heavily into a snow bank. "Hey, what is this boot doing here? There's money inside it! More money. Wow, Gary! This is our lucky day!"

"Who would leave a boot behind on a day like this?" Gary wondered. "This wasn't here when we went out! It's dry on the inside too, so it can't have been here very long. What do you want to bet that lady left it?"

"Lady," yelled Jim, "you forgot your boot and your money!"

There was no answer from the grayish gloom and the boys could barely make out the figure staggering up the steps of the small house at the end of the block. Jim dumped the new supply of coins into his mitten.

"Oh well," said Gary, "we tried to be helpful. Let's leave the boot hanging on the gate. Maybe she'll come back for it. Gosh, she has big feet! I'm freezing. Let's get inside. It'll be warmer, even if it is dark."

# [ CHAPTER EIGHT ]

Gary was wrong. The apartment house was not dark on the inside. Mrs. Jackson, who lived on the main floor, was lighting candles to brighten up the lobby. It looked very cheery.

"Home from the North Pole are you, boys?" she asked. "You'll have to use the stairs 'cause the elevator's not working!"

The climb to Jim's place, on the seventh floor, was a long one and the boys were puffing hard and sweating under their heavy clothing when they arrived. Jim opened the apartment door and called out to his parents. No one answered. Dad was probably shopping.

Mom must have finished her letters and rushed off to mail them. The two boys went inside and removed their winter jackets and boots.

Jim used his new flashlight to find matches. He lit a few candles. Gary dumped the wet money from his mitten onto the kitchen table. Jim added his share. There was quite a pile. The coins glittered in the soft candle light.

"Let's see how much we've got," said Jim. "I'm sure it all belongs to that lady. We should take it to her tomorrow, and the boot too, since we know where she lives."

Gary started to count. "Jim," he shouted, "hand me my magnifying glass and shine your flashlight on the table. This isn't Canadian money!"

They peered at the coins together. Gary became excited, his glasses fogged up and he was forced to polish them with a dish cloth before resuming his study. The boys agreed that the woman in the clumping boots was getting more interesting all the time.

"So, Gary? It's not Canadian and it's not American. What kind of money is this little one?"

"It's incredible, Jim. I saw one of those once, in my Grandpa's coin book," said Gary, as he turned over the smallest coin on the table. "I think this is gold. Shine your flashlight on it again. Yes, I'm almost sure it is!"

Jim became very excited. "Maybe it's worth a lot of money! That lady must want them back. What if it's stolen? These other coins look valuable too. We should show them to my parents. Maybe they should call the cops."

# [ CHAPTER NINE ]

By ten thirty that evening, the electric power was still off, but on the battery radio the hockey game was coming in loud and clear. Gary had come back after supper to listen to the game, and the four hockey fans had demolished the two batches of fudge by candlelight. The score was Rangers two, Leafs one, when the doorbell rang. Jim's mom answered and opened the door to find two police officers.

"Sorry we couldn't come earlier," said the taller of the two officers, after Mom had invited them in. "This has been a busy night, what with the blackout! I'm Constable Wilson, and this is Constable Byrne. What's all this about some valuable coins?"

The two officers examined the money carefully. "We had a report about stolen coins this evening," said Constable Wilson. "I'd like to take these with us, and check the stolen property list." Jim frowned.

"Don't worry," said Constable Byrne. She was shorter than Constable Wilson and had red hair like Jim's. "You will get them back, if nobody claims them in two months time. Where did you find them?"

The boys described the woman who kept falling down but refused to let them help. "I think she lost one of her boots," said Jim. "We hung it on the gate in front of this building. She disappeared into the last house on the left, at the end of the block."

"Thanks," said Constable Wilson. "You boys may have tied up this whole case. Good detective work, I'd say. Do you remember the lady's face? Could you identify her?"

The boys looked at each other sadly. Gary said, "we never saw her face. She had her scarf up over her nose, like us."

"Never mind," said Constable Wilson. "We'll talk to her. Maybe the coins are hers."

"Thanks boys," said Constable Byrne. "We'll pick up that boot, too. If the lady has its mate, that will help prove that she's the one you saw dropping the money. Goodnight folks, and thanks again. You'll hear from us."

Gary, Jim, and Jim's mother ran to the frost covered window after the two police officers left. Hurriedly, each one scratched a peep hole. Unfortunately, with no street lights, it was impossible to see very far. But headlights from a few passing cars briefly lit up the street.

"There they are," shouted Jim. He could see the two officers clearly.

"The tall one with the boot is going up the front steps," Mom called out excitedly. Darkness blanketed the street once more.

Then suddenly, as if by magic wish, the electric power came back on. Lights on the

Kovach's Christmas tree twinkled. The TV joined the radio in its report from New York. "He shoots, he scores!" cried two announcers simultaneously.

"Leafs two, and Rangers two!" shouted Dad. "It's a tie score!" But even that could not take the boys' attention away from the little house on the corner.

Jim held his breath as Constable Wilson knocked on the door of the house with the boot in his hand. It opened and the constables disappeared inside. The watchers stayed glued to their peepholes. Jim could feel every second pass as he and Gary waited for the police officers to come out of the house.

Fifteen minutes later, the door of the little house opened again, and the two police officers led a muffled figure to the waiting police car. The car pulled swiftly away. Excitement over. "Now we can watch the rest of this game," said Jim, running back to the TV.

"Hey! The score is three to two!" yelled Gary "How did that happen? Somebody must have scored while we were busy." And the score was still three to two moments later, at the end of the game.

"I knew the Leafs would win!" shouted Jim.

# [ CHAPTER TEN ]

The next day Jim and Gary went to the rink to try out Jim's new skates. It was mid afternoon before they returned. "Best skates in the whole world, Mom. I only fell down once," Jim was boasting, when the telephone rang.

"Hello, is that Jim? This is Constable Byrne. You and Gary were right. Those coins are valuable. And they were stolen. The woman you saw had stolen the silver teapot from her former employer. And we found a stolen fishing boot too. It matched the one you found in the snow."

"Why the boots?" asked Jim. "They were much too big for her."

"She said she wanted them for her husband," said Constable Byrne. "She tried to wear them instead of her own boots. No wonder she was clumsy! Anyway, the best news is that Mr. Paralovas, the man who got robbed, is so happy to have everything back again, and so quickly, that he wants to give you a reward."

"Wow that'll be great," said Jim. He could hardly believe his ears. "Gary and I'll split it. Gary's the one who knew the coins were valuable. Me and my flashlight, and Gary and his magnifying glass, we make a good team!"

◆

They heard nothing further about the
reward until a few days later, on New Year's
Eve. Gary was helping Jim to finish his jig-
saw puzzle, when the doorbell buzzed.
"I'm not expecting anyone," said Mom. "Who
is it?" she asked, on the intercom.

"Delivery for Jim Kovach," was the cheery
reply, and when Jim flung the door open, a
stranger stood on the doormat. He introduced
himself as Peter Paralovas, the person who
had been robbed. He was a tall elderly man
with a thick grey beard, a fur hat, and an
enormous smile. He handed Jim an envelope.

"A reward for the two young detectives," he announced, as he bowed and swept off his hat. "I'm delighted to have my things back so soon. That women you two caught was my ex-housekeeper," Mr. Paralovas continued. "When I found my silver teapot missing, I was in a terrible state, but those old coins and my best fishing boots are even more special. Thank you, boys."

"Thank you," said Jim, staring at the long white envelope.

"Come in and sit down," said Dad to Mr. Paralovas. "Here, I'll hang up your coat."

"Open the envelope, dear," said Mom. "I'll get our guest a cup of tea, and some fruit cake."

"Hurry up," hissed Gary under his breath. "Don't just stand there! Let's see!"

# [ CHAPTER ELEVEN ]

Jim's hands were trembling so much, he had trouble tearing the envelope open. When he finally pulled out the reward, he could not believe his eyes. In his hand were two crisp twenty dollar bills. He and Gary were both amazed because each of them had secretly believed that the reward was a promise that would never be kept.

At last, Jim sputtered, "Ttttwenty dollars each! Thanks, Mr. Paralovas. Wow! Hey, Gary, what are you going to do with yours?"

"Hmmm. I'll have to think about it," said Gary, scratching his head. "Usually, if I get money that I don't expect, I put it in the bank. My parents have seven hundred and seventy five dollars and ninety three cents saved up for me to go to university."

"That much?" asked Jim. "I save the money that my grandparents in England send me for my birthday. I've got nearly three hundred dollars. But this twenty dollars is going for something special, something we can do this winter. Mom and Dad and I, we've been saving for months."

"Come on, Jim, don't keep me in suspense," pleaded Gary. "What's so special?"

"First I have to check the calendar," mumbled Jim, as he dashed to the kitchen and back. "Yeah! February 16th. The Rangers play here in Toronto!"

"You're all going to buy tickets to see a real game at Maple Leaf Gardens?" guessed Gary. "Neat! I guess I could use my money for a ticket too."

"Yes, yes," urged Jim. "Then all four of us could go."

"Great," said Gary. "I can wear my new hockey sweater."

"Well, three cheers for hockey fans every-where," said Mr. Paralovas. "I'll be away in February, or I would join you. Thank you for the tea and Christmas cake. I really must be off," he said.

"Wait, Mr. Paralovas. What happened to that lady?" asked Gary.

"The police took her into custody. Let's just say that she won't be robbing anyone again soon." Mr. Paralovas struggled into his coat, set his fur hat firmly on his head, and departed.

"You know," said Mom, after their visitor had left, "if that woman hadn't taken Mr. Paralovas' fishing boots, she might have gotten away with the silver teapot and the coins. It was those boots that got her into trouble!"

"You're right," agreed Gary. "She fell right into it! 'Specially when the coins flew out of her pocket and landed under that cedar tree!

And then some more money fell into her boot!"

"And it was the prints of those boots that made her easy to follow," added Jim.

"Well, boys," said Jim's father, "you've had *some* adventure. I bet you can't wait to tell everyone."

"And, we'll have something to write about," crowed Gary, jumping up and down like a jack-in-the box. "Remember, Jim?"

"Yes, Ms. Bardin said we have to write a story about what we did on our Christmas holidays, right?"

"Maybe she'll let us write it together. Hey, Jim, do you think anyone will believe us?"

"They will, Gary, if Mr. Paralovas lets us borrow his boot!"